Mole's Sad Day

Written and Illustrated by
SAVANNAH FIELD

Fulton Books, Inc.
Meadville, PA

Published by Fulton Books 2020

ISBN 978-1-64654-468-4 (paperback)
ISBN 978-1-64654-469-1 (digital)

Printed in the United States of America

Dedicated to her Mimaw-
Sharon London Marcantel

It was a sunny day, and Mole heard the ice-cream truck.

But when he got his ice cream, he loved it so much that he wanted to play with it. But when he played with it, the sun melted it. Mole was sad, very, very sad!

Mole was so sad that he wanted to run away.

But when he tried, his friends caught him.

"Hi, Mole," said Cat.

"Why are you so sad?" said Rabbit.

Mole sighed. "Well, my ice cream melted."

"Oh," said Bird.

"Well, we feel sorry for you."

Dog thought, *Hmmm*. "Well, I know how to make ice cream, and I can make you a new one," said Dog.

"You can?" said Mole.

"Yep," said Dog. "I sure can."

"Thank you so much," said Mole.
"You're welcome," said Dog.
When the ice cream was done, the first thing Mole did was take a big bite.
"Yum, I love it!"

THE END!

ABOUT THE AUTHOR

Savannah Field is ten years old. She lives in Lake Stevens, Washington. She has always loved animals, but most of all, horses. She is an academic achiever, an equestrian, and an artist.

She has been riding horses since the age of four and has progressed into the competition ring in the Arabian Horse circuit in their area. Her new horse Ben, a.k.a. "Irresistible DDA," is a purebred Arabian from Texas and is twelve years old. They have big plans for this year!

Savannah loves to draw pictures in school. She writes stories, paints, and creates clay creations.

Her grandmother is an artist and has been teaching her love of art for many years already. They both worked on this book for over a year during weekend visits. Her grandmother offered to illustrate for Savannah, but she wanted to do it all by herself. With her grandmother's guidance and patience, Mole's Sad Day was born.

Her family have always appreciated her talent, but for some reason on this book, everyone urged them to go full steam ahead and try to publish it!

CPSIA information can be obtained
at www.ICGtesting.com
Printed in the USA
BVHW020109190720
584045BV00001B/18

9 781646 544684